For OZ Who makes his own Rules! Best!

RULES FOR COOL

RULES FOR COOL

DOUGHTRY 'DOC' LONG

56-LONG

This book was printed in the United States of America.

To order additional copies of this book, contact:

Xlibris Corporation

1-888-795-4274

www.Xlibris.com

Orders@Xlibris.com

CONTENTS

FOR

LORI, NIA, AND DJAMILA

"WALK THROUGH LIFE
BEAUTIFUL MORE THAN
ANYTHING,
LOVE ALL THE THINGS
THAT MAKE YOU STRONG"

ACKNOWLEDGMENT AND THANKS

The Geraldine R. Dodge Foundation
The New Jersey State Council for the Arts
The New Jersey Artist Teacher Institute
The Trenton Writers' Guild
Dan Aubrey
Naomi Cullum
Phoebe Davidson
Krishna Gundy
David Keller
Pablo Medina
Peter Murphy
Rachel Simon
Cynthia Mason-Matcho
Shirley Norman
Robert Salup
Eloise Bruce
Nancy Nicholson
Barnes & Noble
Mind and Soul Bookstore
Yusuf Rastafari
Urban Word Café
Cave Canem Retreat for African American Poets
Staff and Students of Trenton Central High School

PHILOSOPHY I

"This," the professor said
pointing to the word 'LIFE' written on the chalk board,
"lasts from the womb to the tomb,
and I guarantee you,
bet your life on it, declare it's axiomatic
no matter how much you squirm or twist
cheat or lie
how rich or how poor
crooked or straight
you will not get out of it alive.
Now
Are there any questions?"
The room was as silent as a graveyard
He was peering over the rim of his glasses.
"Okay, class dismissed."

PROCESS

What's happening
What it is
What it be
What up
What's up
What's going down?
I sat under a tree and listened
To the earth drumming.

'66-LONG

A HISTORY LESSON

some

     seek to

          own the light

  others

     only to

        dance

            in its glow

SAY AMEN

Homeboy Homebrew from Jenkins, Georgia black-red clay. Walked country miles in a stride. Played coon-kane, drank white lightening, smoked jimpsom, carried a high-john root and a black cat's tooth, and was not to be fucked with any day of the week, but especially on a Saturday night. Even the devil contemplated him through leather and smoke. He walked with a limp from a crap game gun shot wound, and carried a purple razor-scar across his right cheek, (a memory of a love affair gone wrong with a whoo-doo woman he crossed in Tennessee). He knew what he wanted and wanted what he took. Low life and low down, one of the Lord's bad boys. Now let the church say, "Amen."

They say that when Amos B. Jones died, there were two angels standing at his bedside, two black angels both dressed in coveralls and work shirts wearing brogans. Folks claim their faces shined like polished brass, so bright that they were almost impossible to look at; they set off a glow that sent a trembling through the room. They just stood there, not moving, not speaking, not giving any kind of sign as to why they were there. Just stood there at the head of his bed glowing. But that wasn't the most bizarre thing that took place in the room where old man Jones lay dying. They say a crow flew through the open window of the room and alighted on the bed post right over Amos' head, right between the two angels. Say it was a crow with a yellow breast and that it had the face of Amos' father, Will Jones who had been dead more than twenty years. Word split both ways, as to what it meant; some called it a bad sign, and others declared it was a sign of redemption for Amos, who had died a renewed and righteous man after almost a lifetime of loose and low-down dirty living.

After a man dies, stories always emerge as to how he lived, and events from his life are spoken of with embellishment or with just plain outright drunken exaggeration. One day after Amos had been layed to rest, a group of his old buddies were reminiscing about him. They say it was he who (in a movie house in Jenkins) shortly after the war, while drunk, had set the town movie house on fire. The story went something like this:

One Saturday afternoon after work, a few of the men-folk of Jenkins would go to the picture show. It cost a nickel and one could see a double-feature, two pictures for the price of one. The main feature was usually a cowboy picture, a shoot-'em-up, and the second feature about some Northern city-slickers caught up in a crossed-up scheme about romance and money. Well, on this particular Saturday, there was a double feature shoot-'em-um-up both starring Tom Mix. Now, if there was a cowboy that ol' Amos was crazy about, it was Tom Mix; his high white hat, dungarees rolled up at the bottom, and his two shiny six guns laying on his polished gun belt. And ride a horse, what you talkin' 'bout!! Amos had been drinking earlier that morning at Ike's Pool Hall. After losing a game or two of pool, he left out of the pool hall (corn whiskey bottle in his hip pocket half empty) and headed to the Prince Movie House. Sometime during the second feature, the cattle rustlers and a corrupted sheriff cooked up a scheme to frame Amos Jones' hero. Tom Mix was accused of shooting a homesteader, rustling his cattle, and setting fire to his house. Amos B. Jones was on the edge of his seat enraged, empty corn liquor bottle lay on the floor near his seat, "You a lie," he exploded, "Mr. Tom ain't had a damn thing to do wid it, wadden I sittin' right here watchin'!!?"

"BLAM!!, BLAM!!, BLAM!!" He emptied his pistol into the high silver cowboys flashing before him on the screen. The movie house caught fire and the drunken Amos, labeled "assassin," was attacked by a mob that beat him, first into a coma, then beyond recognition, then was hauled off to jail. They say he didn't do any time though; claimed he had been affected by the war and something in his head just wasn't right. The patriotism and jubilation after a war victory in the small town had delivered him from doing time.

After that, he moved North where he confronted the factories and the steel machines of the developing cities. And it was there that the machines finally took him under, did him in. The steel galvanizing machines, the open acid tanks, and tar vapors, tied knots in his lungs (that eventually exploded) and sent cancer blooming all over his body. He returned home to Jenkins to die, the ashen sorrow, sagging from his face. It was a year to the day that he lay dying in the back room of a boarding house.

His funeral was held at his mother's church since he himself never belonged to a church. Among the mourners that day at the Holy Cross Baptist Church were his mother, his sister Mae, and her husband Jake, the choir, one or two members of the deacon board, the church mothers, the official mourners, and half a pew of some of his drinking and good time pals. Reverend Haywood's sermon was short; he warned the congregation of wrong doing, the torments of eternal fire and brimstone, and urged them to be born again and seek redemption.

Amos' head lay like a gray stone immersed in the lace and white pillows of the bronze coffin, a slight grin etched on his lips. Dressed up for the first time most folks could remember, white shirt, dark suit and tie. A few flowers and sympathy cards lined the tables at the head and foot of the coffin.

"Didn't look like him to me."

"He looked good."

"They sure put him away nice."

Conversation swept through the small group as they filed out of the church. The final rites at the cemetery, outside in back of the church, were articulated quickly. The weeds and grass shook with the electricity of the July sun and the racket of crickets and cicadas spiked the still air. Two grave diggers in sweat-soaked tee-shirts stood a few yards away in the shade of a maple tree, mopping sweat from the backs of their necks, their shovels lay near their dirt covered shoes. Ice clicked inside a mason jar filled with water as one drank deeply, then passed the jar to the other. They watched until the congregation filed back inside the church for repast. Then they picked up their shovels and walked on strong legs towards the open hole in the ground where the body of Amos Jones lay. A crow flew overhead and barked once. From inside the church, one could hear the voice of Reverend Haywood at the head of the table urging the gathering to say, "Amen."

FRIDAY NIGHT AGAIN

in the house down the street
life abandons itself
america commits suicide
frail ghosts smoke brimstone and curl
in the primitive hurt
in the basement under a blue light they
fire-up another pipe
and chase the smoke genie into the gates of oblivion

and a man named jesus
walks in the alley alone
preaching to stones and bones

in the house down the street
in the basement
abandoned hope murders tomorrow
inhales a dragon
floats in the bowels of never
calls to a vision

it will not see again

mr. jesus pats his foot on the concrete
curses and spits into the diseased wind

in the house down the street
they fly into the earth's lung
gaze into private rooms of eternity and
at night when hell spills over into the streets
the dead will roam the earth
wait on street corners
with eyes lit with questions

mr. jesus hurls a brick at the moon
alarms go off
the dead flee
flying side-ways with crazy wings
stolen from the devil

MOTTO
FOR THE FOLKS

TAKE IT ONE DAY AT A TIME
'CAUSE LIFE TURNS ON A DIME

66-LONG

AT THE BLUE MOON BAR

six whiskeys and a beer
the bar is empty
the town is empty
and we are only here because
there is nothing else to do
nowhere else to go
no one else to talk to
it is raining on a friday night
and we are sitting here on this slow boat
to zanzibar, maybe timbuktu
where people are still awake
this time of night
maybe that's jesus down the street
in the storefront church praying for us
the whiskey runs so fast we can hardly keep up
I move closer (inside your breathing)
speaking to you in chinese
you say something in bantu
the music on my hand
embraces the song on your thigh
the boat rocks
the church shouts
we skim across the night inflamed

like stars fleeing their orbits
untranslated messages   drumming
heading towards timbuktu

ENLIGHTENMENT

In an open field
On a july afternoon
the sun is whiskey
and my head is lit up
with the pungent silence
of wild flowers
If I speak
I will pray
If I pray
I will sing
If I sing
I will become a bird
And fly away

TALKING THAT TALK

I want to know you like orange sunrises in egypt
want to be with you like wind across clover filled meadows
want to tell you like thunder rolling in the distance
want to keep you like rose buds unfolding

I want to hold you like a june sky holds a full moon
want to squeeze you like a stone grows from the earth
want to touch you like pink on satin
want to stroke you like fresh fallen snow

I want to fold you like the curve of a wave
want to spread you like the even hills of africa
want to spin you like a sand storm in the desert

I want to dance you like a shooting star
want to sing you like cornfields in iowa
want to fly you like time goes after time
want to hone you like a crescent moon

I want to move you like still wind chimes
want to turn you like the curve of a peach
want to taste you like the first light of dawn
want to love you like a wheel going around, around and
around

25

A FABLE

It was a hot and humid Saturday night
so hot and humid the birds and trees
sagged with exhaustion from being so perfect.
The devil was sitting in a tub of boiling water,
relaxing, eating a bowl of rattlesnakes and lizard
tongues, and smoking brimstone. He began to wonder
what people thought about him, and what they were saying
about him behind his back.
He called to his servant, who was asleep in the next room
dreaming of beautiful tragedies, and asked him to
get his red suit and pitch-fork, because he was going out
on the town to raise a little hell.
The wind was low.
The moon was high.
The stars were bright.
The people were laughing, and reciting poetry and dancing and
singing, eating sweet potato pies, and growing flowers, and
listening to music, and not doubting themselves, and being
helpful to each other.
The devil became confused and unhappy and went back home
took his red suit off, and tossed his pitch-fork in the corner
and cried, he cried so hard there were stones inside his tears,
that fell to the floor and shattered like a broken heart.

THIS MAN YOUR FATHER

(FOR MY DAUGHTERS: LORI, NIA, AND DJAMILA WITH ABOUNDING LOVE)

this man your father
thin
jazz bent
gray haired and balding
poetry voice
respect him
like him or
dis like him
is what you will
come to like or dislike
about yourself and the world
and that will make you who you are

this man your father
your friend
your blood
your brother

your truth
from georgia earth
the son of history
was who he had to be
to become who he is

what your father
gave to you or
did not give to you
will one day be
what you will give or
not give to yourself and others
what you needed from your father
and what you would have him give to you
give that to yourself

this man your father
the one you have perhaps
scorned in word or thought
knows your frustrations and fears
turn the page
forget it ever happened

what you think of your father
is what others will think of you
is what you will come to think of yourself
yet
who would I be
without you
and who would you be
if there were no me
this man your father

were you a wounded child
I was too

and so were my parents
and their parents
and their parents before them
but who can blame them
for being unable
to change the past

or should we
forgive our parents
and their parents
and their parents
and talk to each other
about fears and joys
pray for each other to be our best
trust each other
believe in each other
stay strong for each other
sit down and eat good food
talk about history our
struggles and victories
laugh and celebrate
sing
even cry together if need be
stand up

get together
we are who we are
were you a wounded child
I was too
this man your father

now put this prayer away
in a safe place
close to the things

you treasure most
and come back to it
from time to time
when there are questions
about why and why
read it again
think about it
be happy
smile

I HEARD THAT

on route one
near down south avenue
across from the big shopping center
around sunset every evening
hundreds of blackbirds
congregate and sit on powerlines
like notes on a music scale
and sometimes while I'm driving
and listening to music on the radio
they look like they be bopping to the music
heads
moving up and down

ON THE STREET OF DEFERRED DREAMS

on the street of deferred dreams
I saw a man hurl a brick at the sky
he said he had no heart
that the wind had stolen it
and buried it in a secret chamber
of the moon
on the street of deferred dreams
a woman was standing on her head
reciting scriptures and eating rusted
nails from a cross
I saw children a hundred years old
drinking history from their own tears
and striking matches to see into
their mothers' wombs
on the street of deferred dreams
I met some who slept all day
and walked to egypt every night
I saw old people
who had turned to stone
talking to ghosts
eating thoughts

from the eyes of fish
on the street of deferred dreams
the winds of change are thin
cold hearted and diseased
there is no music
there are no smiles
I saw the world end and start over again
on the street of deferred dreams

66-LONG

MID-NIGHT INSIGHT

Crickets scraping against low metallic stars
an electric fan hums the gospel
fire flies blink inside silent blades of grass
in a lighted room
on the second floor
the first line of a poem explodes

IF

if in your pocket
you have only a dime
and the dime will not speak
and your pocket cries broke
and the world has caught fire
and you are lost and confused
without a telephone or
fax machine or a slice of pizza
in a jungle that's abandoned of saxophones
and the one you love
doesn't live there anymore
writes to tell you
to learn to slowdrag to the blues
and when the sun has turned upside down
and the moon laughs and flips inside out
and the country you were born in doesn't
speak your language anymore
and when you awake to walk
down the street in a dream and
can't understand what it all means

66-LONG

take a cross, an ankh, some rosary beads
find a cave in a star
stay up all night
and count the wings of angels
that satan has set in flight

WHEN YOU MEET YOURSELF
FOR THE FIRST TIME

it will happen one day
or at mid-day in the afternoon
or maybe one morning   who knows what time
but it will happen
as sure as coming and going
it may happen as a gun shot
or as a flock of birds flick
and scat from tree tops
or quietly like eavesdropping
on a prayer from your own heart   it will happen
and in that vacant utterly clear moment
in a cold and abandoned room of the spirit
in the crowded universe of collected stars and wisdom
you will meet yourself for the first time
and say   with a slight grin perhaps
hello, come in, sit down
let's begin

COLD THOUGHT

row house shacks in the inner city
get cold at night and sag
under winter's chill
make you miss your woman
the need for tender sweet
it's this way in the city
it's the way it's always been
turns a heart to sadness
blues is the mother of sin

HAIKU

Autumn winds raging
Better shut the front door
Money don't grow on trees

66-LONG

A SENSE OF HISTORY

after slavery ended
we embraced freedom and laughed
and gave the children
new names
new faces
new hair
new music
new sunrises
new rivers
and new ways
then told them to remember and trust the
old names
old faces
old hair
old music
old sunrises
old rivers
and old ways

so that they would never become slaves again

2122

UNTITLED

(RE: THE CIVIL WAR IN SIERRA LEONE)

diamonds scooped from the earth's heart
reflect the future and the past
diamonds are sometimes found in africa
where secret men sell them
to buy guns to kill their brothers
men dressed in shadows
shape diamonds into sacred and shiny things
like crosses and rings
where hip american entertainers
who once came from africa, too
buy them, get high
on their own sound and fury
dance on the bones and ashes of ancestors
shouting obscenities into long cool nights
that will one day
come back to haunt them.

41

BIGGER THOMAS

Bigger Thomas is out of the slams
is in a rap group called *fear, flight, and fate*
the video is on all the stations
the CD is selling gold
you can buy it on the internet
it's about the pain of love
and beauty of America

MIRROR

approximately everything you say
is a silver lie
a joke
that you alone laugh at
with your two faces
and opposing views

56-LONG

FACING EAST

before the silence of god and gray river's stone
near earth as old as the grasshopper's eye
the fan chants in latin
of a woman I once knew
who danced on dreadlocked blades of prayer
in a church at midnight
somewhere near the moon
her children baptized in the riddle
of hip-hop machines
I called out to her
she yelled back at me
her words shaking like tambourines
inside a cricket's wing

how well we know ourselves
is what shapes the earth's song
is what gives silence its prayer
she ran from the cathedral
looking back only a moment
then disappeared into the trees

CONTENT

it is october
summer of indians
red and yellow trees
leaves falling into
the arms of egypt
children running
playing games in the park
birds flying in easy flocks
couples walking in the
wine sun holding hands
america on a saturday.
I needed nothing
I desired nothing
possessed nothing
I was happy that I
had lived this long
I was happy of what
the past had made of me
you were the song
the earth was singing
and all that I had
was what I loved

UNTITLED

a man with eyes as wide as death's surprise arrived
with a spot in the home town cemetery
black briefcase
dark suit
midnight necktie undone in haste
shirt collars frightened birds
words and a handshake as cold as december rain
the price list laid out on clean white paper
plan now
less expensive
feel secure
down in the earth won't be as cold
someone who loves you will see to that
save
buy now
a place in heaven
jesus
he grinned.

wind chimes on the front porch swayed like mercy
a storm was making its way up I-95
people were vomiting money
love was held hostage inside a room of mirrors

mothers shoved their children from fast moving dreams
sign here he urged   none of us will get out of this alive
he stopped clicking the ball point pen then handed it to me
my grandmother cleared her throat
from a picture hanging on the wall

66-LONG

ON THE WAY TO KINGSTON

the brown lady in the coffin in the shop window
is from brooklyn
no
zanzibar
but she doesn't know it
she doesn't even care
watching time flip past the window
like books she has never read
sells oils and incense from someplace far away
glues lavender diamonds on her fingernails
walks past the empty mirror again again
she knows someday he will come
bring butterflies from egypt
will have the light wind cupped
in the palms of his hands
cast it against the silence
and it will call her name

DRINKING WITH RUMI

Rumi
Jelaluddin
Where you been
Elusive lyric you
Feeling seer of
Is inside is
Announcer of wine in a flower
Music inside color
Rhapsody
It was all God
All good
Wish I could have had a drink with you
In one of those small clubs downtown
Late one night
Early one moon
The place as empty as a mosque
Except for a couple of women seated at the bar
Throwing eyes at us
And maybe some musicians praying
Inside long blue music, long green music, you know
And we would be talking about poetry and
God and wine and speculating
About cosmological speculations and the meaning of this and that
And the room would be swollen with the fever of freedom and love

49

And you would lean over to me
And say something like
Something way-out hip and deep like
Damn man
What silence played as deeply
As the night has ever been so beautiful
Against the contradictions in the order of this profound
moment
I mean God
Then I'd lean back and say dig it, and we'd slap five
Then maybe you'd get up
Wink at the ladies, dance
Spin around and around so fast
Everyone in the place would get drunk
Then we'd leave maybe
Take the ladies with us
Go sit in the park
Swill some wine
Talk until the sun came up, until the sun came down
Then talk some more then drink some more
And I would say peace
And you would say joy
And I'd say yeah
And you'd say love
And I'd say what
And you'd say wine
Then the ladies would
Jump up and sing
Jump up and say
This is the joy of existence
Then the whole thing would
Start all over again
This time inside flowers
I mean God!

BACK IN THE DAY

our hands were birds
our hands were stones
our hands were light
we were good with our hands then
body punching
jab jab hook
sweet and fast
three punch combinations
like sugar and jesus
left hook slide weave jab
explosive right hand   boom
check
to the mid-section
kidney
under the heart be-bop
going hard to the body
remember the first time man-man and bay-bay went
a whole hour on the corner
by mr. green's store
it was dark when they finished
streets lights had come on
pretty quick hands

striking like serpents
left the flesh scarred and swollen
pain as necessary as baptism
a right of passage
an esthetic of the streets
we were good with our hands
birds
stone
light.

HAIKU

on his way to church
a young boy with a bible
a white butterfly

HAIKU

They took your woman
And then they took your money
Soon they'll have your mind

UNTITLED

love foams from red lights
inside motel rooms on route one
the hideouts
made for love
an hour at a time
or until the sun comes up
jiffy romance the wham bam rooms, wild fire
fake names, fake faces, escapes of ecstasy
cars outside, engines still running
with desire
no words
the couples wear sunglasses
so that they cannot see into each others hearts
a wild scene, animals inside the walls trying to escape

°66-LONG

INSIDE WHEN

of blue watermelons inside silver rain past we danced
love lost in the casino of hearts
back then little richard preached
a-wop-ba-ba-lubop-a-wop-bam-boom
he meant it for all of us who lived
in runover shoes and homemade haircuts
the sweetness of life on a string, a record spinning around and around
life the wild dance
and we got way way down
deep into the night
tomorrow was another day

ADVICE TO A YOUNG MAN

first
> see your reflection in the morning wind

then
> learn the prayers of the people

later
> rebuild the city

'66-LONG

AMAZING GRACE

we were standing in a long line
next to a cotton field where slaves
used to work and pray
we were waiting for the mothership to come
fly us to the new place
our leader had given us all sunglasses
changed our names and
supplied new imaginations and new vocabularies
we synchronized our hearts
and checked our mythologies
the line was so long it reached into oblivion
it was raining faith
the only light came from the leader's mouth
in the distance someone was singing
the song did not have the word "I" in it
when the mothership arrived
we were not allowed to look back
and we pretended we did not see the batteries and cables
connected to the back of the leader's head
being soaked by the blinding torrents of metallic rain

US

like to walk cool
wear hats to the side
dress nice and dap'
talk junk and laugh
and be all right with
each other the earth and
music in the world all around
we just like it like that
that's all
that's all.
jump!

UNTITLED

(FOR LOUIS ARMSTRONG)

blueapple music from yesteralways fell from the sky
a green rooster in polka dot suspenders
a wide-brimmed hat in a yellow cadillac
at church on sunday morning
all of it coming from the same place in the back of my mind
a place near dahomey or sierra leone
blue music always made me dig myself
open the mirror of my heart's secret book
took me to where i was standing
found me in myself looking for myself
fell out of everything i touched
taught me to dance and be still
to trust prayers
recognize love
trust what i could not see
blue music sounded on me
screamed on my emptiness
opened a question

pulled my coat to
what i thought
what i didn't thought
blue music in the soul's garden laughing
counting the wind's mathematics backwards
solid
blueapple music a
green rooster in polka dot suspenders

SUNSHINE

steel-gray march sags
under gray rain
falling from a gray sky
that is filled with gray clouds
splashing on a gray car
i'm in my 50's with gray hair
gray smoke twists from a cigarette that
a man flips gray ashes from
gray birds roost on gray buildings
people rush through the gray rain in gray coats
a gray dog limps through the streets
a gray cat scats in all directions
a man blows his breath into gray hands
gray is the code between black and white
in a world filled with gray and blue
my woman leans over and
whispers she   loves me

MY LOVE

she is as old as the pulse of drums
as young as the first pink ribbon of dawn
she smells like the wine of gardenias
and country rain on summer afternoons
she comes to me in moments i least expect
but always when i need her most
she speaks to me soft and loud
in passion and in rage
comes to me naked and open
or in long gowns of hidden sweet surprise
i can be with no other
can sleep with no other, i've tried
she owns my fire
owns my soul
owns the night i lay down inside of
my mistress
my woman
main squeeze
sugar thing
my lie and religion
my love
poetry

TRAPPED

You are not who you think you are, the one you try to be.
The real you, the one you do not like, the one you are afraid of
Turn your back on
Slam the phone
Keep passing in the mirror without speaking to
That's the real you
Nervous, fake and flawed
Unpredictable and spazed
Knows that any day now you might pull the covers off of who
you think you are
Who you try to be knows
You might scream on who you want to be
Who you trying to be
Because the you you're trying to be
Is like a shoe that does not fit
A hat that's too large
A snap shot of you caught looking the other way
You don't like who you are, and who
You're trying to be is afraid of you.

ATTENTION SPAN

PAYATTENTION
PAY ATTENTION
PAY   ATTENTION
PAY   ATTENTION
PAY   ATTENTION
        PAY   ATTEN
AY   ATT
                  Payattention

'66-LONG

BLESSINGS

(FOR MARION, TOMMASINA AND TALITA)

what thought was i then
breathing next to you
fire on a mission   wind storm
fugitive emotion
a mask needing love but afraid to be touched
a wild man heart deep into what my heart was saying
moving into your song your music
what devil or angel was it that possessed me?
                    us?
i didn't know
i didn't know
i didn't know.
we hurt
and the scar remains in our smile
for the rest of our lives.
what goes around
comes back to us. always.
we danced together once
and changed the world forever.

HOW HOT WAS IT

it was so hot
the wind needed a fan
water was sweating
the sun had on shades
fans ran backwards

it was so hot

churches forgot to take-up collections
cats were chasing dogs
fish bought air conditioners
ice water was drinking a soda

it was so hot

there were no birds flying
ice asked for a glass of water
dictionaries were lost for words
prostitutes sat on church steps

so hot

a woman in a red dress was sweating flowers

67

louis armstrong stopped smiling
possums went to sleep in the middle of the highway
with no shoes on

so hot

the devil got baptized
a frog milked a cow
a monkey met his uncle
a goat laid an egg
a snake fried it
a roach ate it

it was so hot

your mama slapped your daddy
your daddy slapped her back
and they took you to jail, so you could do the time

it was so hot

politicians stopped lying
now you know when that happens
it's pretty damn hot

THIN LINE

pray for me she said.
    no.
i mean
    make love to me.
no.
    wait…
buy me a gold chain.

69

DR. MARTIN LUTHER KING, JR.

(ON SEEING HIM BEFORE HIS DEATH IN
1968)

in the hurricane
in the tornado
in the whirlwind
and chaos
the first thing I noticed
were his shoes   the kind I'd always wanted
hat   sky
clean-shaven mustache
the drape of his pants
over black pointed-toed shoes
dapper-down
veins in his throat
vibrating and bellowing
barked fire and crosses

a fly zigzagged above the podium

OCTOBER BINGE

half a moon is left hanging in a vacant tree
half of who i am is still with you
the other half so drunk i carry my stomach in my head
i smell of cigarettes
beer
sweat
cheap music and the perfume of a lap dancer named jasmine
who whispered in my ear to write a poem about her
and her silver chains
her hand cuffs
green wig
painted eyes
and black whip
when i get home i'm going straight to bed
and i hope to god that i do not dream

'66-LONG

LESSON ONE

It works like this   she said
Removing his heart from the wrapper and
Spinning it around and around on the kitchen floor
Until it turned bright red
        See
                Feel the spin
                       The whirl
                The dizzy
Yes I see I can he said emptiness
Bleeding from his chest onto his shoes
It's called LOVE she said
Only this way
You don't really have to care that much

PAY WEEK

Caldonia dances with her hard head
The hoochie-coochie against the wall
There's a crap game going on in the next room
Sevens fly
The snake's eye
Saturday night fish fry
In the music lies and prayers
Will lay down with each other tonight
Brilliant profanity
Sports a gold tooth

*66-LONG

SPACE WALKING IN THE CITY

(AUGUST 3, 1964 FOR JOHN GOLDEN AND WESTON MURRAY)

This is a poem about space
Inner space and
Outer space
And the space between now and time

It's a poem about the space between old friends

And about finding, knowing, and being with each other
A celebration of being born at the right time

A poem about our children, our mothers
Our fathers, our women, and our dreams
And the spaces they fill in our lives

This is a poem about a spaced-out yet wonderful city
Where our people struggle in the hot syrupy-sweet streets
Trying to find their identities and
Fill spaces between knowing and not knowing
About people caught in the spaces between mind and feeling

It's a poem about cool breezes on central park benches
And horse drawn carriages and lovers and sightseers

And joggers and bikers and skaters and side-walk vendors
And artists and workers rushing home at 5:00 o'clock
And taxi cabs and lonely veterans who have traveled
All over the world moving in the space of the city

It's about people whose language
We don't understand and the spaces between us
That grow wider when they criticize this country
and still praise the countries
From whence they've come

It's about rich folk crowding into spaces
To fill their souls with packaged
History of those they have opressed

It's about the spaces filled
Between King Oliver and Bird
Jelly Roll Morton and Monk
Ma Rainey and Lady Day
The spaces that Miles squeezed light into
And the hypnotic revelations of 15 young trumpeters
Exploding their visions at 2:00 a.m. in the morning
Beneath the streets of new york city

A poem about the space in inquisitive eyes
And the smile of sassy young women following the music
Jazz dancing and winking invitations to spaces in
Loose perfumed arms from sidewalk cafes

It's about us and the spaces

75

Between us
The spaces that make us who we are
That separate us in our wisdom and truths
And our historical fears
The man-spaces that make us uniquely who we are
The treasured spaces that make us friends

And this is a poem about the spaces of sadness
Filling the lives of those we once knew and loved
Who now move in blue trances in and out of days
Lost in spaces outside of life
And how we want to reach across those spaces and
Say to them in clear and certain voices
Hey, I've been there too

A poem about the spaces between God and
Us and our tedious longing
To unfold His glorious mystery

A poem abut the spaces
Between the stars at night and how they
In their journeys fill the galaxies of hope
And about how a white line of truth on the blacktop
Of the new jersey turnpike stretches homeward
At 4:00 a.m. in the morning and

About how some genius of sound on the radio
Showing off on his horn spins revelations

Of how he has filled the spaces in his life

This is a poem about sweet sleep
And the space between sleep and waking
And between today and tomorrow
This is a poem about space

Inner space and
Outer space
And the space between now and time

766-1ONG

TWENTY ILLUSIONS

(FROM A POET'S DREAM JOURNAL)

1

a crow flew out of a tree into a tree
a crow flew out of black man's head
and disappeared into history
the crow flew back then told a story of slavery and trickery
2
a monarch butterfly turned into a leaf, was a leaf
a leaf turned into a monarch butterfly, was a butterfly
3
i was in africa at the time watching garveyites
pack their bags, unpack their bags
time passed
4
smoke spewed from a smoke stack
smoke is standing in the wind at the mouth of a smoke stack
zimbabwe
a long way off

5

a tree was on fire with music
there were no people around to see it dancing
it was dancing because it was free from slavery

6

two loves two times two
shake that thing
you know what you want to do
I like it like that

7

the kiss was in black and white
the relationship in color
the breakup in black and white

8

a witch flew out of my brother's nose one night
and hid under the bed
nights we could not sleep we could hear her drinking moonshine

9

worked in a factory making tools
for the annihilation of explanations
related to why the heart has wisdom too

10

at the bottom of a well in africa
someone was laughing
i was at the bottom of a well laughing
talking back to myself
i never told anyone
call nicodemus

11

pink flesh and a divot of bone and hair
she had jumped to her death they washed the sidewalks
with detergent and hoses
the people walking by
looked up to the thirteenth floor
she was in the shop across the street drinking coffee

12
long-headed black men in white robes
nodding shaved heads in unison to music only they can hear
their heads are watermelons stolen from the full moon
13
the black man is a parable
the end of which has not been written
the black man is a parable
the beginning of which has not been written
the black man is a parable
pages from a book have been torn out
14
a black woman jumped down the throat of the devil
and saw his motives
the devil jumped down the throat of a black woman
and hid there
she vomited him into adam's apple
15
in prison steel and concrete become flowers
even danced with them
forgot darkness
forgot where he was, dreamed the same dream 100 times

16
a blind man laid down to
dream in soft blue sounds
could feel the touch of smells
inside black he felt safe
17
where they lived despair was sacred, was divine
prayed to plastic crucifixes in the dark
worked in technological cotton fields, satan rose to be
the head of the church

18
soul catchers own the night, bend perception out of shape
hide inside glittered trinkets and jaded light
body bandits craving flesh suck the prayers from viruses
19
stand quietly in an open field alone at night
listen and you'll hear the earth sing
you'll never be the same again
now go and bury your old heart
the earth has given you a new one
20
two died in my arms
gray lips frozen against the wings of death
the old man with a hooked finger pulled me
to look inside his mouth and see the oceans there
the young woman, we breathed and squeezed her heart
until the silence from inside of her yelled and laughed
death told us to leave her alone

21
a crow flew out of a tree into a tree
a crow flew out of black man's head
and disappeared into history
the crow flew back then told a story of slavery and trickery

RULES FOR COOL

Book One

        1
become friends
with the color blue
        2
always serve music warm
with everything on it
        3
never say yes on friday
or the first of the month
        4
check out peoples' games
from across the street
        5
only speak loud enough
so that spiders with shades on
can hear you
        6
always keep an extra pair of shades
to wear at night in the house

7
dance, but act like you're not dancing
and when you do, always be cool and in your hump
8
wear clothes that make you look like
one of those jazz dudes
9
be into deep heavy stuff
and carry large intelligent words
around in the same pocket with your money
10
only sing to your woman on weekends
11
stand on the blade of a razor
in barefeet when you turn your collar up
12
know that in the end
love may be the only way out
13
learn how to become invisible
and to see others who are also invisible
14
speak five languages with your eyes
15
know at least one quote by charlie chan or confucius
16
know two songs by james brown
17
stay free, fly
learn the mathematics of the drum
18
when you meet satan
acknowledge his red suit and coat
but keep your own tightly buttoned

19
rebuild what you have taken apart
then begin again and remember
20
know that blasé blasé
woof, woof, woof
at the right time and place
is sacred
21
know that the wind is your cousin
be yourself
remember where you came from
if you're lost or forget
ask your cousin the wind
22
only smile when
you are in pain
23
cool recognizes cool

24
the cool which is spoken of
is not the real cool

MAN-MAN

man-man rents sleep in a second
floor room in ms. rose's house
walks up and down the street on a mission
assigned to him by the mothership
dresses in black
and wears those tee-shirts with bright colored pictures
of famous black people like tupac and wu-tang
carries a cassette player and headphones
talks back in rhymes to the tapes
while he walks to the beat
he won't say nothing to you
if you don't say nothing to him
won't steal
respects people's property and
don't mean no harm to nobody
don't mess with him he won't mess with you
he just be walking and talking back to those tapes
he don't drink and he don't get high
word is something happened to him one time
he got sick
that's why he act like he do
just a young man from the inner city with the blues
dropped out of school

can't find a job
no skills to sell
needs something good to happen to him
a job
a friend
a lady
someone to unlock his head
redirect his mission
keep him from walking the streets so much
talking back to the tapes
and waiting for the mothership

BLUES FOR WES

twelve hours of slow midnight rain
a rich man wets his thumb
counts his blessings again
bob marley and a fleet of angels
on the radio prayed while
six demons shot craps
across the black topped night
and a woman with a plastic heart
practiced throwing knives in the dark
po' boy cries jesus on his way home
from the funeral of a best friend

i remember how on our corner late at night
we talked all night about philosophies
and big words and how to pull women
trying to stand bent-cool like miles
and be deep in the funk like monk
quick hands we went hard to the body and dreamed
of one day being in the blow-wig pages
of ebony and jet
brown boys from georgia, life a solo trumpet
chanting in the blood
we balanced the lopsided world on awkward finger tips

87

our fathers worked in factories, our mothers
cleaned houses on the outskirts of town
we had nothing, needed nothing, wanted much, wanted nothing
lived in a world turned gray from believing
in the unseen
world made of tears older than a griot's memory

the world called us, used us
we saw the game
took our falls stood up broken
and went back to living again
we knew the blues and paid dues
cool one, hip, 'dapt like that

we grow old, and tired of habits and passions
of cigarettes
of books
of music
of words and talk
and of long midnight highways
whipped with rain

yet we lived long enough
to thank all of the angels
who led us to places
we did not always willingly want to go

INTRODUCTION TO DREAM CYCLE I

PART I

In a room without walls and without a city I awake and find a nun standing over me chanting a mantra in Swahili. She makes the sign of the cross in the air over me. Boils a praying cloth, then serves me the tea. People in the room, familiar faces from times and places before, huddled together, processed hair, combed to the shoulders, toothless, they grin sideways, in the corner is an auction block, money and whispers change hands. The nun covers my eyes, turns my head away, I struggle to turn back. She warns, "No, Wait. Not now, it's revelation, it's revelation, don't." She begins to cry. I turn back. She has taken her clothes off. "Call the coin while it is in the air," she says. Two prostitutes come into the room dancing and singing. They sing, "...too much love, too much love, nothing kills a brother, like too much love." They take their clothes off and make love to the nun. I go to the window and outside a girl standing on the corner is passing out bibles and lottery tickets. In the room the prostitutes and nun are dressed in evening gowns sitting on white horses. One of the prostitutes jabs a needle into her fist, the nun sips white powder into her brain. "Call the coin while it is in the air," she says. People outside have shaved their heads, walk up and down the streets covering their eyes. Syncopated shouts, "No wait, it's revelation, it's revelation." Chants roll through subway tunnels, "…too much love, too much love, nothing kills a brother like too much love." The nun takes me in her arms rocks me, rocks me, the sun shatters glass on the river. A clock on the walls cannot remember its language.

PART II

The next morning the sky is vacant blue balanced light. The wind is humpbacked pink. Someone knocks at the door but there is no one there. When I return to the room he is sitting in a white tuxedo, top hat, gloves and walking stick. Smoking a $99.00 cigar filled with cocaine and Egyptian love songs. He takes out a violin and plays "Amazing Grace." We sit at a roundtable. He takes out a pocket handkerchief and lays the issues on the table; bible, gun, lottery ticket. I protest, try to go back to sleep. I want to dream reality. My girlfriend and my cut buddy come into the room, hand me a sheet of paper, my obituary is written on it. They smile and start slow dancing. I protest. They say I'm paranoid. He juggles the issues and beckons for me to come sit at the table. "These are your choices." He thumbs through the bible, pulls the trigger of the gun and there are no numbers on the lottery ticket. Trees outside ask if I've been baptized.

PART III

We were driving down a dirt road, when suddenly, we came into a clearing and a huge mansion appeared. There was a sign outside in front. It read, "Suicide Camp, Death is a Good Thing." It was painted in bright bold colors and there was a garland of flowers and a dozen of helium filled pastel balloons floating above it. The gatekeeper was impeccably dressed, clean shaven and the color of his skin was dark brown, the color of the cherry tree bark. He had a calm, sober look about his face. Little wind stirred. Birds darted through the trees. The sky was even and perfect. "Hello," the Gatekeeper staring off into the distance, smiled and said, not looking us in the eye, "Take your bags?" I woke up. The phone was ringing.

MYTHOS FOR MILES

(FOR MILES DAVIS)

a man and a horn
a sound
a style and an attitude
a spirit and a way
a motion, a cool
a kind of prayer is gone
darkness and darklight.

a man eats the sun
sleeps
and dreams history.

a man eats the moon
sleeps
and dreams the otherworld.

a man eats the stars
sleeps
and dreams heaven.

in the morning he awakes
memorizing the journey on his horn
the sound is incandescent sky.

766-LONG

ON THE BACK ROAD FROM PRINCETON

JUNE 23, 1997

what kind of night is this
the sky is drenched with stars
the moon is so full
it might roll from the sky
lovers burn and turn in each other's arms
magical things are in flight tonight
cool breezes have wine in them
i hope i never get home

MARTIN AND MALCOLM

Martin and Malcolm were walking down the street one day
When Martin turned to Malcolm and began to say
"We need to integrate, the jim crow laws of separate and equal
Are only a disguised plan to keep out colored people
To keep them thinking they're less than man
America is our birthright, and we must take a stand"

Now Malcolm listened intently and he cleared his throat and said
"We are Africans in America, from our homeland we were led
Those thoughts of integration, were placed inside our heads
We need to do for self, let them keep their hateful ways
Let's have our own in unity, and build for blacker days"

Then Martin slowed his pace and countered
"Now back to Africa we can't go
The ways and paths there we no longer know
It's here we've got to make our stand
Realize our dream and implement a plan"

"Now brother wait a minute," Malcolm held up his hand in jest
"The dream of America was never meant for us
Why integrate into a house on fire
Let's defend ourselves, and take our people higher"

Then Martin, his brow, grew a little weary
Reflecting on mad dogs and fire hoses
And nonviolent marching as a theory

And Malcolm in his silent wit
Thought in America we can't fit
And confusion in the minds' of people
Would never see us treated equal

They continued their walking down the street
Then stopped for a moment their trudging feet
And pondered deeply what each had said
While quietly a sniper man
Picked up a gun, and aimed it
                          coldly
                             at
                                     their heads.

HIP-HOP BOYZ

Caps turned south
Dipped in baggy madness
Step to radios and videos
That rhyme like
Automatic weapons
Trying to forget the
Walls they have cursed and torn down
Must someday be rebuilt

HIP-HOP GIRLZ

On their way to parties
Dressed in confused flesh
Eyes would do anything
To be chosen as neon stars
Wanna party all night
And spin so fast
They forget the lies
They have told their mothers

97

COUNTRY FOLKS

say old man Shadrack
come back a possum
see him nights
come scuffling from a hole he dug
underneath the house
low to the ground fat belly
dragging the dust, long rat tail
tip curled up moving behind him
he'd go far as the edge of the field
may lack he hunting something
all the time eyes cocked back and set
on the porch of the house
silver grin on his face teeth shining
'gainst the moon
say he come back like that after he died
to watch out for his wife and kids
dogs wouldn't nair bark
full moon stood still
wind come to a hush
he'd squat there at the edge of the field wait
'til folks got up from the porch and went inside
get ready for bed

soon as the lights go out in the house
here he come again creeping
back underneath the house
go back in his hole
none of us never said a word about it 'til now

766-LONG

THE SEDUCTION

enjoy the blues she said baby
you know despair is a deadly sin
it weakens the spirit
takes countenance from the soul
a natural enemy of hipness
smile and go with the flow of shadows
embrace fear and step into the darkness backward

then she slapped him
placed his hand on her breast
wiped a tear from his sleeve
and they walked into the blue
jazz filled night
her perfume a galaxy
of slow saxophones shook
the drunken applauding stars

and he turned the music up louder
and asked her to dance
and they danced   they danced
in the infinite mellow wine of the blues

SOMALIA 1992

a death wagon comes twice a day
to villages in somalia
once at sunrise and again just before sunset

men with masks over their faces
tie the bodies in burlap bags and
stack them like bundled sticks
in the back of rusted cattle trucks

masked drivers haul the dead to fields where
grave diggers sweat maggots
to keep up with the body count

death's grin is embalmed
on the faces of the living
while the smell of starvation screams in the air

a soldier standing nearby polishes his gun
spits in the black dirt
adjusts his sunglasses

766-LONG

ADVICE TO A WRITER

(FOR RICK WILSON)

If you should sit
In a chair at a desk or a table
To write on a machine or on paper
And find yourself falling
Through the chair
The paper
The machine
The desk
The floor
And down through the earth
Into an endless tunnel
That leads nowhere in the present
The past or future
Do not panic
Or become afraid
Only struggle
To get back out of the tunnel
With as much evidence as possible
To make the reader believe that
What has happened to you is true

PROVERB

let me see you dance
and I will tell you
who you were as a child
let me see you dance
and I will tell you
how the bird in your soul
seeks its freedom

766-LONG

FOR STUDENTS

be all-that and
who you are now and always
walk and talk what you say
and feel for yourself
and those you love

       stay
       amazed even about morning stars and
       lights at night
       whenever wherever you awaken
       and find yourself changed

believe
in the invisible remembered song you
were born and step to every day
forget tomorrow's gloom
yesterday's moon

       remember life
       is
       how you YOU
       dance

to the music moving
      in the mirror
      of your own mind and heart

stand straight up
be positive but real
and keep your jab sharp

766-LONG

AT THE IRON MAN'S GYM

pumping iron up to the ceiling
some tattooed and bearded groan and sweat
after pushing concrete and black top
fifteen miles down route 1 in the middle of july
            "a man should be able to bench press
            his weight plus his age" iron
slams against iron punctuating a command
a six pack and pizza at home in the fridge
a woman calling from the next room
the news on tv reports the condition of man
and the final scores
            "country's headed to hell in a handbasket
            you ask me" iron
silver mirrors in a steel quagmire throw back illusions
the treadmill hums and whirls beneath my feet
the pulse rushes
walking
walking
walking
trying to get to egypt

F R E E D O M

this photograph is in black and white
grays merged perfectly in late afternoon
freedom is standing on the corner of blues
and memory street in a torn coat dancing in the wind
no shoes no hat trousers rolled to the knee eyes
pulled back like full moons
mouth yelling something invisible
oh freedom

you used to be so cool, smooth like a
turn around jump shot
used to wanna be like you, walk like you,
dress ivy league, talk like you, you were jazz and
the nitty-gritty bow-dimp the pimp sho-nuf the
next flight to the real thing my ace spoon-coon
freedom, you usta been so cool.
I would actually seek you out
stay up late in pursuit of you
up before dawn wondering if you were
going to walk by my way today
now, you like this, on the corner,
to see you this way. Freedom

107

someone turns the news on
the radio the tv I can't remember which one
and the color of the photograph changes from
black and white to color
to a vicious red frightening screaming red
and the news says 46 year-old James Byrd, Jr.
was chained to a pick up truck and dragged to death
in Jasper County
East Texas body torn into 75 pieces
Along a country road

today is june 7, 1998
two years before the turn of the century
around here in this neighborhood
people are talking about making ends meet
and about working together
to make the community a better place to live

the photograph turns to black and white again
and now freedom, like this
on the corner of blues and memory street
hurts me to my heart

WHAT DO THOSE X's ON THEIR HATS MEAN?

(SEVEN POSSIBLE ANSWERS, AND THEN SOME)

X
MALCOLM X
    x-ray
    x-pose
    x-plode
X the hawkman's eye

X
MALCOLM X
    the unknown
    criss-cross
    cross
X razor sharp

X
MALCOLM X
    x-pert
    x-pel
    x-pand
X walked his talk

X
MALCOLM X
    cancel
    obliterate
    ten
X saw the future rise

X
MALCOLM X
    x-cite
    x-ample
    x-hale
    x-act
X do for self

X
MALCOLM X
    intersection
    free
    -out of
    -plexus
X by any means

X
MALCOLM X
    x-purgate
    x-clave
    x-spend
    x-change
X saw through the jive

109

TO FIND A HEART

went to new york yesterday to buy a new heart
my old one had stopped feeling and seeing
caught the 9:30 am straight over to new york city
walked right into the heart store
and the heart store man said, "yes, can i help you
mister man, you know this here is new york city
and we aim to please, so what can i do for you today?"
i know this is new york city, cause i came here on the train,
and paid for my ticket, and the conductor punched it,
and yelled out "'last stop, new york city," '
and i got off the train and walked right in here to this shop.
so yeah, i know this is new york city.
told him i was looking to buy a new heart, my old one wasn't
feeling and seeing just
how i thought it should. "fresh out of hearts, just sold the last
one yesterday before
closing. got an order coming in in about about two weeks,
first of the month.
take your name and phone number and call you when they
come in."
he was matter of fact.
"if you had come yesterday, you'da caught the sale, lowest prices
on hearts on the

east coast. april is when we sell most of
our hearts anyway."
i turned to leave, walked towards the door. resentment turning
in my head like a whirlwind.

"got some real fine eyes, just got them in this morning, they
sees real good,
they sees change coming, sees backwards into mysteries, and
forward into the
seeds of time sharp and clear. they're domestic-made i believe. not to mention
how they see through people's games. eyes make you see
your mistakes
before they happen." "nah," i moaned back over my shoulder,
and moved toward the door.
"okay, then how about some feet, give you a real good deal on
some new feet
built for country walking, but they got new york style.
key, key, key, key, key, key," he laughed from behind his teeth.
"these feet take you anywhere you wanna go, walk fast or
slow,
run with them if you want to.
now if you don't want new feet, and just want to keep your
same old eyes,
then i know a man like you could use a new pair of hands,
can't just sell you
one though, got to sell the pair. these hands is strong 'n steady,
soft and hard,
work with them or rub you or your lady soft. one touch with
these hands and you'll
never have to wonder 'bout where your woman is. good hands.
imported from the ivory coast." i shook my head no.
"okay what about these, just got them in, yesterday," he reached
under the counter

and came up with a hand filled with ears, "can't beat these, make you hear so damn
good, you could hear
a mouse piss on cotton during a thunder storm, hear day break, time pass, a dollar bill fall in the snow. if you take the
ears, i'll throw in a pair of legs supreme, top of the line
legs, thinking about getting myself a pair for my next birth-day."
"no, no, that's alright, it was a heart i was looking for, it
was a heart i came in here for, a heart i needed for seeing and feeling."
i left the store, boarded the train back to jersey. the train was packed, standing
room only. had all of these people been to new york looking for a heart?
after the first two stops on the train, a seat became available. i sat
next to a little old brown-skinned woman whose bags rested on her lap and
next to her legs on the floor. she had gray hair, a kind round face,
someone's grandmother, someone's nana. her eyes were the color of robin's
eggs, a pastel blue. "pretty ain't they?" she smiled into my face, she was toothless,
"a fox give 'um to me, one night i caught him stealing eggs out the hen house down
in athens, georgia, he turned my eyes blue. pretty ain't they?"
i nodded my head
yes, half afraid to say no, and at the same time wanting to encourage her mystery.
she said nothing else. i laid my head back, closed my eyes to get some rest.
the train hummed through the dark tunnel of night, the crowd of passengers swayed

back and forth in the thick, tedious silence. i nodded
into a soft sleep. sometime later, i felt a hand touch warmly on
mine, my eyes
raced open. she was starting to gather her bags, "never could
find that heart could you?"
"what??", i drew back in surprise, "that heart you was running
around over there
in new york looking for all day today."
before i could answer she intruded,
"boy," don't'you know this here ain't your heart," she pointed
to her chest,
"this here is your heart," she aimed a withered brown finger to
the side of her head.
"this here is your mind, she pointed the same finger back to
her chest. "don't worry,
lots of folks gets them mixed up, lots of confusion in this world
i'll tell you that,"
she giggled. "now 'cuse me, this here is my stop," i stood up
and she moved past me,
both hands gripping bulging plastic shopping bags.
"yeah, lots of confusion in this here world today" she giggled
her way into the
flowing crowd moving towards the exit of the train. she never
looked back.
i never saw her again. never went back to new york looking
for a heart.
the train zoomed towards trenton.

A POEM FOR SOME WHO SURVIVED

and now you're 50
but you could have been dead
or double-crossed somewhere
caged for life
needing something
as simple as sunlight or laughter
or had a bullet in the brain
or shot-out on white powder walking to and fro
down crazy streets without eyes

but you saved your life   survived
heart
Islam
raised fist
your children
your mother
the woman who taught you
to touch love
a flashed back insight
line from a poem
a song remembered
an instant of utter clarity

don't doubt it for a minute
it was all real, all good
you walked your talk
stood your ground
a distant runner
believe it
and you've lived to see it come around again
what message will you whisper to the young ones
stay low
run silent
strike quick
    search deep
live

TOWARDS A DEFINITION OF ART AND MAN

(FOR THOMAS MALLOY)

Light runs, and speaks darkness
darkness runs, speaks light
line speaks void
void speaks line
vanishing point speaks nearness
nearness speaks vanishing point.

Canvas and artist struggle in dialogue,
eye captures illusions
Fire in a brush stroke,
colors explode. Light.

Light is only light
because darkness is
darkness only dark
because light is.

They say you drew a black line
in the red dust of a blue Carolina afternoon
and the line spoke and said something, meant something.

Say you drew an indigo line in yellow dust
of a pink Carolina afternoon
with a green stick that
a purple God had given you.

and the line spoke
and the dust spoke
and the colors spoke
and God spoke
and you spoke
everything spoke and asked

What is the color of truth and beauty?
Just what is the shape of beauty and truth?
And you drew a turquoise line in the ocher dusk
And it replied in infinite, brave dimensions.

REMEMBER THIS

(FOR DJAMILA, NIA, AND LORI)

perfect
in your born isness
as perfect as darkness
pressed against the night
like blue music spinning out of
the first light of day
as perfect as the sphinx
pyramids
mathematics
astrology
the first thought of god
the instinct of flowers
the synchronicity of rain
wind sun and stars
seeds and the ocean's flow
dig yourself
see yourself
step into the world and

always remember this
never forget this
you are perfect

766-LONG

NEW YORK, NEW YORK

If you ever go to new york, new york
you will fall in love
with someone or something
some rhyme some reason
a time, a season
hard zoom just like that
fall in love and
the abracadabra of the big apple
the spell of blue-silver wind
springtime, the heartrush, the beat
above life beneath life
the swarm of lights
that never sleep, buildings and pavement
the poetry goes on forever
dance or sing you
will feel rich and
walk as if you knew where you were going
in new shoes
throw your head back and laugh
turn your eyes face to the ground
new york will whisper secrets to you
that will come true the very next day

it could happen at broadway and 42nd street
or maybe downtown, or up in harlem
on the east side or west side
at 3:00 a.m. in the morning
or at breakfast or noontime
new york is a city of thrills and spills
heartbreak and wildest dreams
you will never get to see all of it
or get to know its deepest secrets
yet if you ever go
to new york new york
you will fall in love
with someone or something
some rhyme or some reason
hard zoom bang just like that

766-LONG

THE CAPITALIST

he takes his eyes out and puts them in his wallet
puts them in his back pocket
folds them between the breathing of dead presidents
the dead presidents smile and wink at him
they whisper that all salvation is here
that this is beginning and ending
he stacks his anxieties on the table and counts them
by tens   by thousands
one-thousand, one thousand-ten

        tell me things that money won't buy
        and I'll sing you a song
        that will make you cry,

one-thousand-forty, they are counting the dead in ethiopia
in harlem, detroit, atlanta, johannesburg, el salvador,
in nicaragua, in palestine, in iraq, in iran and in
trenton, new jersey
they count the dead until the numbers turn to rain
then to sand, then to oceans and then to vacant sky
two-thousand-fifty
two-thousand-sixty
two-thousand-eighty
one-hundred ninety-nine thousand

he takes his eyes out and puts them in his wallet
puts them in his back pocket
folds them between the breathing of dead presidents
the dead presidents smile and wink at him and he
winks back

766-LONG

TWELVE FACES OF GOD

1

A cat crouches
Watching a squirrel
A spotted dog is watching the cat
The eye of God is wide

2

A coin spins
After falling to the floor
It is spinning so fast it is still
The room is inside the heart of God

3

In the bell of a horn at midnight
Jazz pours from the light of the moon
The entire city is intoxicated
God solos in the blue dust

4

At night winter's chill
Clicks on the heater
Soon it will be warm in the house
Outside God is walking through the trees

5

Snow drifts knee deep
The world is as quiet as bellowing smoke
Weather reports on the radio
The face of God appears in the clouds

6

People sitting on their porches at night
Summer hangs like a giant watermelon
God whispers, a cool breeze

7

In the holy-ghost church
They shout in the aisles
And speak in tongues a joyful noise
God struts in the ringing tambourines

8

In the organ drenched sympathy of the church
The family is gathered for the funeral
And beneath the veil covering the widow's face
Lay the silent shadow of God

9

Fishing alone in a backwoods stream at dawn
The moment bends and quivers
I reel in
God is in the eye of the fish

10

A chorus of children singing
Voices believing in what they sing
Like in a field of flowers
God, the wind connecting the heart to this

11

A sudden spring rain
Like in the backrooms of hell
Floods pour through the city streets
Inside the rushing water
One hears the breathing of God

766-LONG

12

Watching a sunset explode
Across the lake
Water and sky become one
And we are hurled and transformed
Inside the glory of God

NOW

when jesus lived in harlem
wore a conk and sported gators
and collard greens grew on trees near the euphrates
and money like water flowed like gin
and it was saturday all the time
and love, a ripe melon, at the touch
bloomed into succulent sweet

when we were old
but time was young
when we were music
and the earth our song
when sisters were queens
and stars their thrones
when this was right and
that was wrong
when we were kings
and poets saxophones
how beautiful black was then

then time belched illusions and the sun went out
history was held hostage in a convex mirror
slavery the middle passage

127

cotton fields diseases mad dogs assassinations
drugs
inner city blues
genocide
a crack in time
how did we get so far gone
where do we belong
sleepless
riding the moon back and forth to Africa
gold chains tangled in our hair
and some nights weary with questions
I dream of Betty Shabazz trembling and berserk
mumbling sacred things inside the pandemonium of fire
we watching
this is how it is at the turn of the century
everything has come true

red lights blinking walk
don't walk